THE NIGHT I WAS CHASED BY A VAMPIRE AND OTHER STORIES

THE NIGHT I
WAS CHASED BY A
VAMPIRE AND OTHER STORIES

KAYE UMANSKY

Illustrated by Chris Mould

Dolphin Paperbacks

First published as four separate volumes by
Orion Children's Books:
The Empty Suit of Armour first published 1995
The Bogey Men and the Trolls Next Door first published 1997
The Spooks Step Out first published 1997
The Night I Was Chased by a Vampire first published 1996

This collected edition first published
in Great Britain in 2004
by Dolphin paperbacks
an imprint of Orion Children's Books
a division of the Orion Publishing Group Ltd
Orion House
5 Upper St Martin's Lane
London   WC2H 9EA

Text copyright © Kaye Umansky 1995, 1996, 1997
Illustrations copyright © Chris Mould 2004
The right of Kaye Umansky and Chris Mould
to be identified as the author and illustrator of
this work has been asserted.

A catalogue record for this book
is available from the British Library

Printed in Great Britain
by Clays Ltd, St Ives plc

ISBN 1 84255 289 9

www.orionbooks.co.uk

Contents

The Empty Suit of Armour

SQUEAK

In a castle on a hillside
On a cold and moonlit night

The mice
    behind
    the wainscot
Got a very nasty fright…
And an owl up in
    the rafters
Gave a sudden,
    startled hoot
As an Empty
    Suit of Armour
Raised its arm in a
    salute.

Its helmet swivelled slowly
With a harsh, metallic squeal.
It tested out its knee joints
Just to see how they would feel…
Then it brushed away a cobweb
And it stood up really straight,
And clanked across the hallway
With a strangely jerky gait.
The castle doors swung open
(In the creaky way they do)
And the Empty Suit of Armour
Very squeakily marched through.

rattle
squeak
clunk
clank
grind grind

The night was cold and frosty
But it didn't seem to care.
It stomped across the courtyard
With a most determined air.

It didn't stop to grab a hat,
Or bother with a coat.
  The drawbridge slowly
  lowered
    And it marched across
    the moat.
      It set off down the hillside
(Which was really rather steep)
Giving headaches to the hedgehogs
And deafening the sheep.
A poor old shabby shepherd
Sipping soup upon a rock
Spilled the contents of his thermos
Down his shabby shepherd's
  smock –

Dropped his crook into a crevice
And his sandwich in a stream –
Then bolted like a rabbit,
With a startled little scream.
At the bottom lay a forest
Just as dark as dark can be
With a hundred hungry predators

Behind each bush and tree.
There were wolves and wily weasels,
There were vipers,there were voles,
There were ferrets, there were foxes,
There were things that lurked in
    holes…
But the Armour marched on by
    them,
Making such a fearful racket
That no one liked to be the first
To jump out and attack it.

At the far end of the forest
Was a quiet country lane
Which led to a wee village
(Little Romping-In-The-Rain).
Just a quiet little village,
With a peaceful little brook,
The sort of place where folks
Retire early, with a book.

Up the lane the Armour clattered
With a bold, defiant rattle,
Past a torn and tatty scarecrow
And some very puzzled cattle.
A farmer sipping cider
In the local village inn

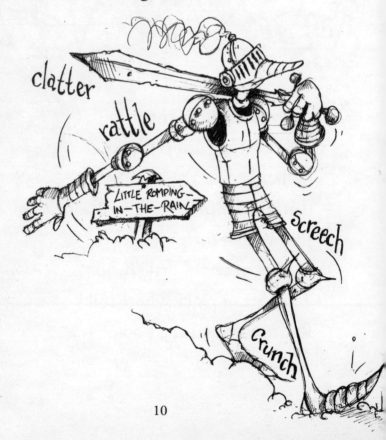

clatter

rattle

LITTLE ROMPING
-IN-THE-RAIN

screech

Crunch

Turned his head towards the window
At the fast approaching din.
Then the farmer spied the Armour –
And his eyes grew even wider,
His face went pale and with a wail
He fainted in his cider!
The lights came on in cottages
And people stared in fright
At the Empty Suit of Armour
Who had spoiled their early night.
A dog came up to sniff it
With its ears laid low and flat.
Then it backed away stiff-legged.
No. It wouldn't mess with that.

cresh
squeal
clanK

rattle

squeak

The Armour kept on going,
Past the churchyard and the mill,
And it left that little village
And marched onwards, up the hill.
All that night it kept on going
With a stiff, relentless tread
Till the sun filled the horizon
And the moon went home to bed.

Now the road became a thoroughfare,
A place of squealing brakes,
Of motor cars and lorries
Bearing Mr Creemy's cakes…
Of juggernauts and caravans
And motorbikes and scooters
And little grey-haired grannies
Honking madly on their hooters.
But the Empty Suit of Armour
Simply plunged into the fray
And marched right down
   the middle,
Just assuming right of way.

The road led to a market town
That buzzed with cheerful chatter
As the early morning shoppers
Stood about and had a natter.
But there was a heavy silence
At the shrill cry of dismay…
"There's an Empty Suit of Armour
And it's heading right this way!"
The crowds fell back respectfully
To let the Armour through,

Alarmed, but rather curious
To see what it would do.
And this is what the Armour did.
It reached a sudden stop.
It turned around quite slowly
Then it went into a shop…
And there it bought an oil can
And proceeded to anoint
Every nut and bolt and rivet,
Every shrilly shrieking joint.

And when at last the job was done,
It set the oil can down
And smoothly – slickly – *silently* –
It marched right out of town…
Back to the ruined castle
On that high and hilly ground,
Where it glided through the open
  doors

Without a single sound.
Then it took up its position
With its back against the wall.
Just an Empty Suit of Armour
In a dark, deserted hall.

So if you're ever walking
On a cold and moonlit night
And you hear the sound of
    marching –
Do not run away in fright.
Just nod and smile quite pleasantly
And show no consternation…
For it's just a Suit of Armour
On a quest for lubrication.

The Spooks Step Out

It was midnight in the fairground.
There was nobody in sight. The gates
   were locked securely, with a bolt.
The horses on the roundabout
Had knocked off for the night,
And the Ferris Wheel had rumbled
   to a halt.

The swings were hanging motionless.
They did not even squeak,
Suspended from their gaily painted
   posts.
Then – suddenly – the Ghost Train door
Swung open with a crrreeeaaak…
And out into the moonlight stepped –

The Ghosts!

The first out was
   the Skeleton,
Long and lean
   of limb.
His bones beneath
   the moon were
   white as snow.

He was followed
by the Mummy.
There was no
mistaking him.
He was tightly
bandaged up,
from head to toe.

Next out was a Lady
In a very fancy frock –
She had an air of dignity and charm,
(Though if anyone had seen her
They'd have got a nasty shock –
She was carrying her head beneath
    her arm!)

And last of all, a tiny Ghost
Came flapping into view,
"Hey, hang around, you rotters! Wait
    for me!
It isn't fair to leave me there!
You'd better take me too,
I'll report you to the R.S.P.C.G!"

"All right, gang," said the Skeleton,
"Now, here's the master scheme.
We have a go at everything in sight!

We'll try out every ride, and eat
A mountain of ice cream,
We're going to paint this fairground
    red tonight!"

"Quite right," agreed the Lady
With a sullen little pout,
"We've been stuck inside that train
    for weeks and weeks.

All that haunting's really daunting.
We deserve an evening out.
It'll put a bit of colour in our
    cheeks."

"Let's start off with the
   Roundabout!"
The Mummy cried with glee,
"The Roundabout is always
   lots of fun!

Last one on's a cissy,
And I bet it won't be me!"
And he dashed across the fairground
    at a run.

The Mummy chose a motorbike,
The Skeleton, a scooter,
The Lady chose a reindeer with a
    sleigh,
The Little Ghost decided
On a steam boat with a hooter
Which he honked in a relentless
    kind of way.

The Roundabout began to turn
And soon was spinning fast,
"Oh mercy!" wailed the Lady, "not
    so quick!"

They all felt rather dizzy
When they tumbled off at last,
And the Little Ghost complained of
    feeling sick.

They took him to a soda stall.
He drank a fizzy drink
And got a lot of cuddles from the
    Mummy,

Then he ate six sticks of candyfloss,
All sugary and pink,
And declared he felt much better in
    his tummy.

"I'm feeling in the mood for bumps,"
The Skeleton remarked,
"The Dodgem cars are parked just
    over here."

The Little Ghost responded
With excited little jumps,

And the others shouted gaily,
"Good idea!"

They piled into the little cars
Of yellow, green and red,
And had a most exciting high speed
    chase,
And they had a lot of pile-ups
'Til the Lady lost her head,
And retired a little crossly from the
    race.

The Mummy saw the Hoopla Stall
And thought he'd try his luck,
    saying,
"Skill is what you need to throw this
    thing."

He won a little goldfish
And a yellow rubber duck,
And a hairy scary spider on a string!

Then the Lady won a coconut!
The others loudly cheered.
"Good shot, old girl," the Mummy
    proudly said.

"I'll carry it," the Skeleton
Politely volunteered,
"You've already got your hands full
    with your head."

Next they tried the swing boats
Where they really let off steam,
Up and down and to and fro they
    travelled.

The Little Ghost decided
It would scream and scream and
    SCREAM
And the Mummy got a tiny bit
    unravelled.

Then they tried the Helter Skelter
Which was quite a big success.
The Skeleton went backwards, for a
    dare.

He landed rather badly
In a jumbled, bony mess,
And it took a while to work out what
    went where.

They bought themselves some ice
    cream
And some burgers in a bun,
For the time had come to have a bite
    to eat.

They sat upon the grass
And had a picnic (which was fun)
And the Little Ghost spilled ketchup
  down his sheet.

And then – at last – the Ferris Wheel.
It rose into the sky,
Supported by a flimsy-looking
    frame.

I'm frightened

"I'm frightened," said the Little
    Ghost.
"It looks so very high."
But he went and clambered on it just
    the same.

They held each other tightly
As the giant wheel went round,
And everything beneath looked very
    small,

They screamed so very loudly
As they plunged towards the ground.
Said the Little Ghost, "I don't like
  this at all."

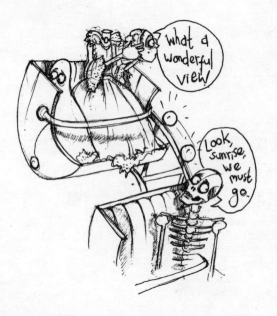

But the view was most impressive
When they reached the very top.
Said the Lady, "This is really such a
  thrill!"

"Oh dear," remarked the Skeleton.
"I think it's time to stop.
The sun is coming up beyond the
    hill."

Sure enough, the sun was rising.
Very soon it would be dawn.
It was time to hurry back and board
    the train.

"That was lovely," said the Little
    Ghost,
And added, with a yawn,
"Though I'm much too tired to do it
    all again."
"What a night!" remarked the
    Skeleton.
"You're right," the others cried,
"It really has been such a lot of fun."

The carriage door swung open
And they tiredly climbed inside
(Not forgetting all the prizes they
    had won.)

That day, the poor old Ghost Train
Was sadly under-used.
All the passengers complained that it
  was boring.

For instead of all the cackles
And the howlings and the boos…
There was nothing but the sound of
    ghostly snoring!

The Bogey Men and the Trolls Next Door

Hello! I'm Fred the Bogeyman.
I live beside the bog
With my bogey wife and kiddies
And my faithful bogey dog.

Now, this is Mrs Bogey
In her baggy bogey frock
And her big, black, bogey bovver
    boots,
Posing by a rock.

(When it comes to breaking rocks
  up,
Mrs Bogey is the guv.
Her name is really Beryl,
But I always call her "luv".)

Here are our bogey children –
Daphne, Bert, and little Douggie…

And here is Baby Bogey
In his bogey baby buggy.

And this is Snot, our Bogey dog.
(We've taught him how to beg.)
He eats a lot of Bogey bones
And sometimes bites your leg.

We're a happy little family.
We lead a quiet life,
Just minding our own business
And avoiding stress and strife.
Yes, I'd say we were contented.
Or at least we were before
That very fateful evening
When the Trolls moved in next door!

We were sitting down to supper
With our bowls of bogey stew
(Which is gooey, rather gluey,
And quite difficult to chew) –

When a knock came on our cavern
   door.
I said, "Who can that be?"
And a voice like grating gravel

Very boomily said
"Me!"

I opened up the door a crack.
The Trolls stood just outside.
They were rocky. They were cocky.
They were weighty. They were wide.

**"Hello! We're your new
      neighbours,"**
Boomed the biggest one. **"I'm Dave.
We've come to introduce ourselves.
We're in the next-door cave."**

**"This here's my good wife Dolly.
This is Colin, Mol and Polly...**

**"And here's our trollish baby
In her teeny trollish trolley.**

55

"And last, not least, meet Tiddles,
Our charming trollish cat.
I wonder, could we step inside
And have a friendly chat?"

I simply stood and stared at them.
I did not say "How do?"
I did not say, "Do come on in
And have some bogey stew."

I glared. I bared my *teeth* at them.
I don't like trolls one bit,
And wanted to be really sure
They were aware of it.

"I'm sorry," I said coldly,
With my baddest bogey sneer,
"Us Bogeys do not like you Trolls.
We don't want Trolls round here.

"You Trolls make rotten neighbours.
You hold a lot of raves.
You do not bin your rubbish,
You never paint your caves.

"You don't control your children.
You like to scream and fight,
You play loud Trollish music
Very late into the night.

"Well, that is what I've heard, and
    I'm
Quite sure that it is true."
And I firmly shut the door
    on them
And went back
    to my
    stew.

SLAM

Well, that was the beginning.
From then on, things went downhill.
Between us and our neighbours
Fell an atmosphere of chill.

And, as the weeks and months
    went by,
Things slowly got more tense.
The children pulled rude faces
Across the garden fence.

The cat and dog were
    enemies.
They did a lot of spitting.

The wives were
    coldly critical
About each other's
    knitting.

59

And me and Dave would shake our
 fists
If ever we should meet
(When we'd been to shop for
 groceries)
Accidentally, in the street.

The Trolls held noisy parties
And us Bogeys would complain.
But they'd laugh right in our faces
Then they'd do it all again.

They invited their relations
For a sing-song every week,
And bellowed anti-Bogey songs,
Which was an awful cheek.

Their children broke our windows
With their heavy Trollish balls
And at night,
   they took their
   hammers out
And hammered
   on our walls!

Us Bogeys got our own back.
We would sneak on out at dawn
And dump our Bogey rubbish
On their tidy Trollish lawn.

We muddied up their washing
And trampled on their flowers,
Then acted most indignant
When they came and trampled ours!

We pinched their pints of lava
(We stole them from the crate) –
We wrote anti-Troll graffiti
On their nice new garden gate.

We smothered all their doorknobs
With Bogey superglue.
We had to scare them off,
    you see,
For that's what
    Bogeys *do*.

We were sitting down to breakfast
Eating Bogey toast and jam,
And our darling Baby Bogey
Was out dozing in his pram.

(We often leave him out there
In the garden, where it's sunny,
Blowing Bogey baby bubbles
And burbling to his bunny.)

"I'll go and check the baby,"
Mrs Bogey firmly said.
"I think he might be sleeping.
I'll just pop him in his bed."

And she strode into the garden.
Then we heard a frightened shout…
"Help, everyone! Come quickly!
Baby Bogey has got out!"

It was true. His pram was empty.
What a very nasty shock.
And over by the open gate
(Which we forgot to lock)…

We saw little baby footprints
Which we stared at, all agog,
For they led in the direction
Of the dreaded Bogey Bog!

The Bogey Bog! The Bogey Bog!
A place of mud and murk,
All bristling with Danger signs
And snakes, and Things that Lurk.

A stagnant stretch of quagmire,
Very desolate and grim.
No place for Bogey babies
Who have not
   been taught
   to swim!

Just then, we heard a startled scream –
And, to our great surprise
The Trolls next door came running
   out
With wildly rolling eyes.

"Have you Bogies seen our baby?"
Came the chilling Trollish cry,
"Our baby has gone missing!"
"Ours has too!" was our reply.

"They must have gone together,"
Dave the Troll then grimly said.
**"We had better go and find them.
Will you come and help me, Fred?"**

What a frenzy! What a panic!
We were well and truly worried,
And down towards the dreaded Bog
Us Trolls and Bogies hurried,

And we quite forgot to argue,
And we didn't fight or brawl.
This was a time of crisis –
All for one and one for all!

At last we reached the Bogey Bog,
Our dreaded destination –
We were worn out to a frazzle
And quite drenched in
    perspiration…

And there we spied our babies
With mud up to their eyes,
Paddling in a puddle,
Busy making muddy pies!

We simply stood and looked at
  them,
So happy in their game.
Then we looked at one another –
And we hung our heads in shame.

The time had come to call a truce
And try to make amends.
From that moment onwards
We became the best of friends.

Now the children play together
And they have a lot of fun.
The wives sit drinking coffee
In the garden, in the sun.

Dave lends me his mower.
I lend Dave my axe,
And when we meet out shopping,
Well, we clap each other's backs!

The Trolls still hold their parties
And they like to sing at night –
But us Bogeys get invited too,
So that is quite all right.

The fence between our gardens
Fell down the other day –
But we haven't put it up again.
We like the fence that way.

Everything is peaceful now.
No more need for war.
Life is so much better
Since the Trolls moved in next door.

The Night I was Chased by a Vampire

I was walking one night in the
  mountains,
My fingers were blue with the frost.
I stood in the snow.
I thought, "Where shall I go?"
It was late. It was cold. I was lost.
I wasn't sure how I got there.
I'd been to my aunty's for tea.
But my sense of direction was faulty
And I took a wrong turn. (Silly me.)
The forest was dark as a dungeon.
I couldn't stay there, or I'd freeze.

I couldn't just stand
With my head in my hand
And the snow coming up to my
    knees…
But how to get out
Was a matter of doubt.
Straight ahead?
    Up or down?
        Left or right?
I couldn't decide.
Then I suddenly spied
Through the trees, in the distance
– A LIGHT!

It came from a tumbledown castle
With turrets and towers and spires,
I hurried right up,
Thinking "Soup in a cup!
Warm water! Thick blankets! Hot
     fires!"
The castle was smothered with ivy.

There was moss on each crumbling
    wall.
It was, I suspected,
Quite badly neglected.
Not what I'd expected at all.
But with knocker in hand
I took a bold stand
And I called, in a confident way,
"Open up! Here's a lost, lonely
    traveller,
Who's looking for somewhere
    to stay!"
From within, there
    came shuffling
    footsteps.

The door slowly opened a crack.
"Well, hello there," I said.
"Any chance of a bed?
And a bath? And a bit of a snack?"
I suppose you would call him a
    butler.
(Though no other butler I've seen
Was built like a sack of potatoes
With eyes quite so piggy and mean.)
He was badly in need of a haircut.
It hung to his shoulders like rope,
Not to mention a scrub
In a scalding hot tub
With a broom and a big bar of soap.
He stared in surprise
With his little pig eyes
Then he scratched his great stomach,
    and laughed.

Then he gave a sly grin
And said, "Come right on in."
So I did. I went in.
(Which was daft.)
The hallway was shrouded in
    shadow.
Dark tapestries reached to the
    ground,
Cold faces stared out from old
    paintings.
Their eyes seemed to follow me
    round.
The biggest hung over the fireplace,
I paused for a moment beneath.
This painting was not like the
    others.
It followed me round with its
    teeth!

"Who's that?" I enquired of the
  butler,
"That chap with the fangs in his
  face?"
He hissed, "'tis the master!"
And hobbled off faster.
And I had to run to keep pace.

"So tell me, kind sir," I persisted,
"This master of yours. Is he
   here?
Does he stay out of sight?
Will I meet him tonight?"
"Well, you might," he replied with a
   leer.

Through corridors, narrow and
   winding
We hastened, in deepening gloom.
Then he set down his candle,
Took hold of a handle,
And said, "This is it. Here's your
   room."

The bedroom was most uninviting,
The cobwebs were thick overhead.
There were shadows that capered in
  corners
And a saggy old four-poster bed.
"It's charming!" I cried,
(Well, all right, so I lied,
But there's no harm in being polite.)
He gave a brief shrug,
Gave his forelock a tug,
Then he grunted and wished me
  goodnight.
But the night wasn't good. No, it
  wasn't.
The blankets smelled badly of
  mould

And I needed to visit the bathroom.
(I told you before, it was *cold*.)
By the flickering light of a candle,
I hastily rose and got dressed,
And I stealthily slipped from my
    bedroom,
And boldly set forth
    on my quest.

I walked down the echoing passage
Not knowing which way I should go.
Then I came to a crumbling stairway
Which plunged into darkness below.
I followed it down to a dungeon.
(I shouldn't have done, but I did.)
And there – shock of shocks!
I discovered a box –
Yes, a long wooden box with a lid!

Then the lid of that box began
    rising!
I let out a horrified shout.
I went cold, I went hot,
I was stuck to the spot…
… *As the man called The Master*
    stepped out.
"Well, good evening," he hissed.
"What a pleasure.
So glad you popped over tonight.
It is such a rare treat
To have folks round to eat.

You will join me, I hope, for a bite?"
I did not like the way that he said it.
I did not like the gleam in his eyes.
So I did the one thing I could think
   of.
I turned and I ran. (Which was
   wise.)
I raced up the twisting old stairway
With the speed of a runaway horse.
From behind came the voice of the
   master:
"Hey, you! Come on back!
You're first course!"
I raced through the crumbling castle.
The master was hot on my heels,

Insisting I join him for dinner.
I ignored his pathetic appeals.
He chased me down stairs and
through hallways,
He chased me up high and
down low,
In the whole of
that crumbling
castle

There was nowhere that we didn't
  go.
I did what I could to outrun him,
In fact, I was gaining a bit –
Then I turned a sharp bend
And I reached a dead end.
  There was nowhere to go.
    This was IT.

I was trapped like a rat in a corner
I had to escape him – but how?
I had no time to beg,
He caught hold of my leg
Which he p-u-l-l-e-d...
LIKE I'M PULLING YOURS
    NOW!